I've Been Working on the Railroad

I've Been Working on the Railroad

Nadine Bernard Westcott

HYPERION BOOKS FOR CHILDREN
NEW YORK

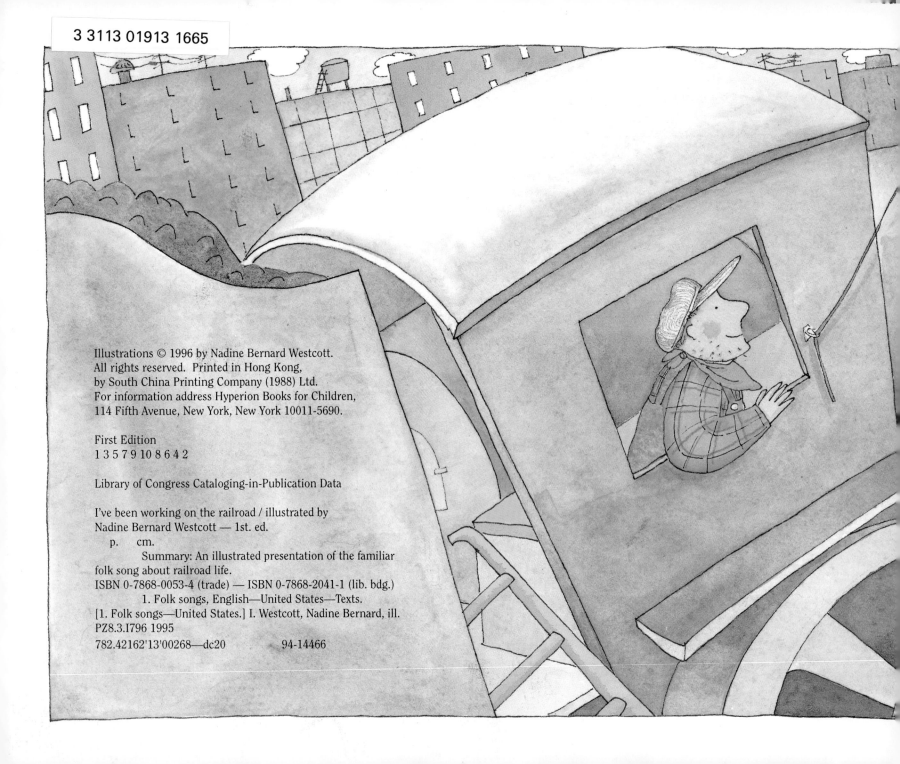

Illustrations © 1996 by Nadine Bernard Westcott.
All rights reserved. Printed in Hong Kong,
by South China Printing Company (1988) Ltd.
For information address Hyperion Books for Children,
114 Fifth Avenue, New York, New York 10011-5690.

First Edition
1 3 5 7 9 10 8 6 4 2

Library of Congress Cataloging-in-Publication Data

I've been working on the railroad / illustrated by
Nadine Bernard Westcott — 1st. ed.
     p.   cm.
          Summary: An illustrated presentation of the familiar
folk song about railroad life.
ISBN 0-7868-0053-4 (trade) — ISBN 0-7868-2041-1 (lib. bdg.)
          1. Folk songs, English—United States—Texts.
[1. Folk songs—United States.] I. Westcott, Nadine Bernard, ill.
PZ8.3.I796 1995
782.42162'13'00268—dc20   94-14466

For Willy

I've been working on
the railroad

All the livelong day.

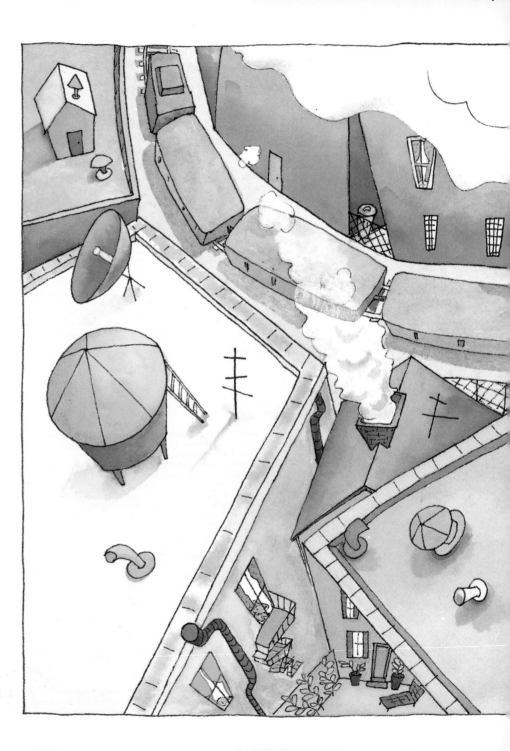

I've been working on
the railroad

Just to pass the time away.

Can't you hear
the whistle blowing?

Rise up so early in the morn.

Can't you hear
the captain shouting,
Dinah, blow your horn!

Dinah, won't you blow,
Dinah, won't you blow,
Dinah, won't you blow your
horn, horn, horn?
Dinah, won't you blow,
Dinah, won't you blow,
Dinah, won't you blow
your horn?

Someone's in the kitchen
with Dinah.
Someone's in the kitchen
I know-o-o-o.
Someone's in the kitchen
with Dinah,
Strummin' on the old banjo . . .

And singing, *Fee-fi-fiddlee-i-o,*
Fee-fi-fiddlee-i-o-o-o-o,

Fee-fi-fiddlee-i-o,

Strummin' on the old banjo.

I've Been Working on the Railroad

The origins of "I've Been Working on the Railroad" are uncertain. It is thought to be modified from a levee tune sung by black railroad workers in the late nineteenth century. Little is known about its oral tradition, although it may have been based on older work songs of riverboating days.

The earliest known date for the song's publication is 1894, in the eighth edition of *Carmina Princetonia*, a college songbook. The song's omission from the previous edition supports the idea that it was not widely popular prior to the early 1890s.

The song grew in popularity in the twentieth century—especially among barbershop quartets in the early 1900s—until by midcentury it was a facet of camp life for American children in all fifty states. And it remains so!